Magical Mayhem

Part Two
To Prevent Chic Costumes

Emily Martha Sorensen

Also by Emily Martha Sorensen

Standalones:
Black Magic Academy

Fairy Senses:
Fairy Eyeglasses
Fairy Compass
Fairy Earmuffs
Fairy Barometer
Fairy Pox
Fairy Slippers
Fairy Lunchbox
Fairy Icepack

Dragon Eggs:
Dragon's Egg
Dragon's Hope
Dragon's First Christmas

Comics:
A Magical Roommate
To Prevent World Peace

The End in the Beginning:
The Keeper and the Rulership
The Fires of the Rulership

Trilogy of a Teenage Werevulture:
Trials of a Teenage Werevulture

The Numbers Just Keep
Getting Bigger:
Twenty-Four Potential
Children of Prophecy

Magical Mayhem:
To Prevent World Peace

Short Story Collections:
Worlds of Wonder

Picture Books:
Tabby, Tabby, Burning Bright

To Prevent Chic Costumes

http://www.emilymarthasorensen.com

To Frederik Vendelin,

longtime fan of the comic,
reader of my other books,
and Patreon supporter.

Chapter 1
The Desperation

Quiet and stillness drifted through the night. Chronos slumbered softly, savoring the rarity of a peaceful somnolence.

"It's been fifty-eight hours, and I still haven't changed my mind!" a voice screamed.

Chronos jerked awake, her heart pounding wildly. She spun to her left side to look at the door to her bedroom, but Kendra was already on her way out.

SLAM!!

Chronos lay there in the darkness, her heart pounding from the shock of being jerked awake. Her eyes ached from exhaustion, and the clock beside her glowed 4:15.

Doesn't she ever sleep? Chronos thought in numb disbelief.

"See you in an hour!" the unwelcome voice called.

Chronos plucked her digital clock off her bedside table, gripping it in her tense fingers. *Four am.* She glowered at the clock as if that would change the facts. *That makes five hours in a row she's done this.*

The first time had been at 11:40, exactly an hour after Chronos had gone to bed to end the former magical girl's latest argument. The second time had been at 12:55. The third at 2:06. The fourth at 3:07.

From the living room, Chronos heard a quiet *thump*. It sounded like someone jumping onto the couch to catch another comfortable hour of sleep.

Chronos's eyes squeezed shut. What was with her insane and incredibly unwanted houseguest?

Maybe this was normal for magical girls who defected to villainy. Such occurrences weren't common, and Chronos had never paid that much attention to them.

She knew someone who did, though. Someone who was an expert in them.

I could ask Rhea to . . .

She cut off the thought viciously. *NO!*

If there was one thing worse than an unwanted houseguest, it was her older sister. It had been five years since they'd last laid eyes on one another, and Chronos wanted to keep it that way.

A traitorous thought drifted across her mind.

Except . . . there's still no chance of Kendra leaving anytime soon . . .

Chronos smashed the alarm clock into her bedside table, feeling sick and angry. Sure, she couldn't see futures that she herself was involved in. Sure, that meant there might be some possible future in which she convinced the former magical girl to leave. But she'd tried everything that she could think of, and it had just made the girl all the more determined.

The first thing she'd tried, of course, was to tackle Kendra and shove her out the front door. The pest had easily broken loose, apparently much stronger in human form than your average magical girl.

"Is that all?" the teenage girl had asked casually. "I've had arch-nemeses who did much worse than that. It's not like I've only trained while transformed."

Chronos had clenched her fists and promised herself to try again a few hours later with the power of surprise on her side.

But that hadn't worked much better.

"Really?" Kendra had asked, dodging as Chronos dove into a wall. "Why wouldn't you assume I'd be on my guard against that?"

The Desperation

Chronos had rubbed her head, and sworn to try again later.

The third time had been just as unsuccessful. And the fourth time. The fifth time, she had finally succeeded, seizing the unresisting former magical girl, shoving her out the front door, slamming and locking the door, and leaning against it in relief.

Kendra had teleported back in. "Are we done with that game now?" she'd asked with a bored look on her face.

Two days later, Chronos was starting to fall apart at the seams.

She thrust her tangled blankets aside, twisted her bedside table lamp to turn it on, rummaged through the drawer, and came up with a pad of paper and a mechanical pencil. Then she started scribbling in large, blocky print.

how to regain <u>peace</u> <u>and</u> <u>quiet</u>

- throw kendra out
    she'd teleport back
        steal the watch?
            how would she get back home?

That's hardly my problem, Chronos told herself fiercely. *She showed up her where she wasn't welcome. Let her find her own way back home.*

Without thinking, she added a second bullet point.

- ask rhea for help

She immediately scribbled it out, furious with herself for even thinking of it. To remind herself of just how bad an idea that was, she added:

NO WAY!!

Biting the inside of her cheek, Chronos quickly moved on. She had to figure out something. Something. Something. Surely there would be some way to get her houseguest to go away.

- explain to kendra that she needs to leave
    tried this. <u>will not listen!</u>
- call or telegraph kendra's family
    with what? don't have those machines
- move somewhere else myself
    she'd follow me
- steal the watch back

Chronos paused at this idea. The former magical girl was sleeping right now. If she snuck into the living room, she could unbuckle the watch from her unwanted guest's wrist, put it on her own wrist, and take off herself. The pest wouldn't be able to follow her, and, well, Chronos didn't really have any possessions that she was attached to.

Of course, stealing the watch back and stranding the pest here would be a nasty trick. But following Chronos to her home had been a nasty trick, too.

The more Chronos thought about it, the more she liked it. True, it would be a nuisance to replace her books and find a new place to live, but that was nothing money couldn't fix. In fact, in a show of graciousness, she could even continue paying for the pest's groceries so that the pest could stay here indefinitely.

It was such a perfect plan, she couldn't believe it hadn't occurred to her earlier. Being forced to interact with someone wearisome for two days had exhausted her even more than mere lack of sleep, it seemed.

Yes. Of course that was the right thing to do. Let the former magical girl have her apartment. She could go somewhere else.

Smiling to herself, Chronos added,

should try again

underneath the bullet point about explaining the situation to Kendra, just in case. But she was confident that this would work. All she needed to do was get the watch off someone who was sleeping for one second and teleport away. How hard could that be?

The Desperation

Chronos reached under her bed and pulled out her fluffy bunny slippers, the ones she'd had since childhood that were now too tight and had holes on the bottoms, and squeezed her feet into them. She shuffled across the carpet and opened the door, which had squeaked two days ago but which Kendra had oiled on her first day here, and padded across the hallway to the couch in her living room.

The former magical girl lay stretched across it, eyes closed, chest rising and falling slowly. Her arm with the watch dangled off the side of the couch, loose and unguarded.

Perfect, Chronos thought smugly.

She reached out softly, ever so softly, her fingers brushing the tip of the wristband —

A hand jabbed across her throat.

"That's mine now, soothsayer," Kendra hissed, eyes wide open.

"Do you sleep at all?!" Chronos exclaimed.

Kendra pulled her arm back, but kept it hovering by Chronos's throat. "Lightly."

"I need you to leave," Chronos said through clenched teeth. "This is my home. You're not welcome here."

"Some home," Kendra said succinctly. "It was a pigsty before I cleaned everything."

"I *liked* it that way!"

"You mean you were lazy," Kendra corrected.

"No, I mean I liked it that way!"

"Impossible," Kendra said, sitting up and stretching.

Chronos made a dive for the watch, but Kendra yanked her arm away and shoved it behind her back, using the couch cushion behind her to shield it.

Chronos made a growl of frustration.

"Really, soothsayer, don't be so stubborn," Kendra said. "We're meant to work together. We'd be a perfect team."

"I have no interest in being part of a team!" Chronos exclaimed.

Kendra shrugged. "Neither did I, originally. It grew on me. Teams can accomplish far more than one individual alone, and we both have goals we need the other to accomplish."

"I have no goals at all," Chronos snarled.

"Yes, you do," Kendra said calmly. "You want to stop having nightmares about bad things. I eavesdropped on you while you were sleeping the first night. You talk a lot in your sleep."

Chronos gritted her teeth.

"Meanwhile, I want to save the world," Kendra said reasonably.

"Did you not learn anything from what I told you?" Chronos demanded. "If you'd just stop trying to save the world, maybe it wouldn't need saving!"

"Yes, it would," Kendra said calmly. "Somebody else is bound to rise up and take my place. You've proven that your power can predict that and prevent that."

"My power can give me nightmares and apparently tremendous inconveniences named Kendra," Chronos muttered.

"Precisely," Kendra said, not looking the least bit bothered by the insult. "That's why we need to work together."

Chronos folded her arms and glared. "If you want to be a villain now, whatever. I really don't care. Go get a job as a Deathwave minion. If you perform well, you can get promoted and eventually become an arch-nemesis in your own right —"

"Thanks, but no thanks," Kendra said coolly. "I know how the Deathwaves work. I want to save the world, not make it a more dangerous place."

"By being a villain," Chronos muttered.

"Precisely." Kendra smiled. "That's why I need a teammate who is both a villain and not."

"I'm not a villain at *all!*" Chronos shouted.

"Knowing how to save the world and choosing not to act on it? Sounds pretty villainish to me."

Chronos spun around and stormed back to her bedroom.

"See you in an hour!" Kendra called after her.

Chronos slammed the door to to her bedroom, flopped on her bed, and seized her pad of paper and pencil.

She added to the two bullet points she had just attempted, heart pounding in rage and indignation.

- explain to kendra that she needs to leave
    - tried this. will not listen!
        - should try again
            - STILL WILL NOT LISTEN!

- steal the watch back
    - wears when she's sleeping
        - light sleeper
            - did not work at all!!

At the bottom, in extreme frustration, she wrote in all caps:

HOW DO I GET RID OF THAT GIRL?

Chronos stared at the list, wanting to fling it against the wall. This was worse than before she had dreamed about the future Avenging Angel. Worse! At least before, she'd had privacy during the day. Now she had a permanent houseguest!

Her eyes fell on the second option she had written, the one she had scribbled out.

No! Chronos thought, burying her face in her knees. *I like that it's been five years! I don't want to see Rhea's new store! Even an unwanted houseguest can't make me go back!*

The pad of paper seemed to stare back at her with its lack of answers and its many dead ends.

Chapter 2
The Sisters

Rhea hummed to herself as she designed her latest outfit for a magical girl. It was one of her favorite challenges, designing something classy enough to keep her reputation as a high-end fashion designer intact, and yet slightly . . . dull.

Magical girls who cared enough about appearances to hire a professional to design the costume for their magical girl form or their next power-up tended to be the perfect targets for her favorite hobby.

She finished it off, adding a flourish of ruffles and little puffed sleeves, the current most popular fashion for ten-year-old magical girls in Paris, and quickly ran down the checklist of items her customer had asked to have included.

Pleats in the skirt. Check.

Knee socks with ribbons on them. Check.

Super duper high heels. Check.

Hair ribbons for her pigtails. Check.

A pink, purple, and turquoise color scheme with no plaid in it, unlike her original costume, which she was no longer happy with because her older brother had made a fake version and worn it on Halloween to make fun of her and it had been the most embarrassing thing ever. Check.

The Sisters

Rhea smiled to herself. She knew exactly how she would have made this costume stunning and distinctive, but she wouldn't do that for the magical girl version. Oh no.

Gleefully, she reached out for her lightbox and began to trace the design onto a new sheet of paper, adding the small touches that she knew the perfectly-fashionable-but-very-generic costume needed. A few spikes here, a red underskirt there, a slightly darker color scheme with a few dabs of black in just the right places to make the soft pastels seem vibrant . . .

A knock came at the door, startling Rhea from her colored pencil reverie.

"Madam!" her assistant called. "There's a fashion disaster downstairs in the lobby."

Rhea sighed impatiently. This was why she'd hired an assistant: so that she didn't have to deal with customers unless she personally felt like it.

"So what?" she called back. "Get rid of it!"

"I can't!" her assistant's voice protested.

Rhea felt her eyes narrow. Minerva wasn't usually so helpless. "Why not?"

"It claims to be your sister."

Rhea leapt out of her chair and burst through the door, running down the stairs to the customer floor of her shop. She didn't even stop to tell Minerva to please tuck in her tail while in her shopgirl uniform, although she made a mental note to speak about it sharply later.

"Chronos!" Rhea cried, flinging her arms wide as she ran through the curtain from the room marked *Employees Only.* "How's my baby sister?"

A rumpled mess of absolute disaster awaited her. There was hair that clearly had not been brushed, a once-white-and-now-greyish T-shirt coated in wrinkles, a pair of pajama bottoms with sheep on them, and, in a new low, her sister was wearing bunny slippers. The same bunny slippers she'd had since she was six years old.

". . . Still unable to dress herself, I see," Rhea said. "Did you have to wear that in public?"

"I don't have the watch," Chronos muttered. "I couldn't just teleport in."

Rhea paused. That was interesting information. She wished, not for the first time, that she could observe scenes from the past that her sister had been involved in.

"Oh?" she asked hopefully.

Unfortunately, Chronos didn't elaborate.

"Did you have a reason for coming, or are you just here to drive all my customers away?" Rhea snapped, turning towards the curtained entrance to the back room of her store.

"Want me to leave?" Chronos demanded.

Rhea drew herself up to her full height. "Don't take that attitude with me! You're the one who wore *that* out in public in Paris, of all places! You're the one who didn't show up at our parents' funeral last year!"

"They died trying to kill a bunch of thirteen-year-olds," Chronos muttered. "I didn't feel like paying respect to that."

"Ah, your sanctimonious 'principles,'" Rhea said acidly, waving her hand. She pushed through the curtain at the back of her store, certain that her sister would follow her and thus be out of sight of customers outside. Sure enough, her sister did. "If you're here for money, forget it."

"I was hoping for advice to get rid of an ex-magical girl," Chronos said flatly. "I've got a defector in my home that I can't get rid of."

"You've been harboring *defectors?*" Rhea burst out, unable to contain her joy. She spun around. "Chronos, that's wonderful!"

Her little sister's narrow-eyed glare appeared to disagree. "Well, I suppose it beats killing children."

Rhea sighed. Apparently her younger sister had not yet seen the light . . . or rather, the darkness. It was really quite embarrassing to be related to someone who was so unwilling to be helpful to the rest of the Olympian villain family. While she herself was not particularly well-loved by Great-Uncle Nico, his animosity had merely come from her attempted coup to replace him six years ago, a perfectly respectable thing for a villain to do.

Deciding that prolonging the argument would do no good, Rhea plopped onto the stool of her designing desk that she kept in the back room. This was where she made adjustments to costumes while customers were present. *Real* customers, not the magical girls she charged a pittance to outfit as a hobby.

All around them were the mannequins covered in spiked or shredded outfits that were waiting for their customers to pick them up just as soon as they broke out of prison. One was for a minion who hoped that a change of costume would earn him a promotion in the Deathwaves. One was for a brand new boss who hoped to cow her minions by wearing twice as many spikes as they did. One was a black cloak with stars that Rhea planned to charge double for because she knew that villain could afford it.

Her personal favorite right now was for a homunculus mage from the Eritai world who had newly arrived on Earth and hoped to pass as a magical girl. It was hopeless, of course, because sooner or later she'd get caught — only magical girls could transform, so it was silly to pretend to be one of them. Still, Rhea applauded the effort, and the situation had sounded so amusing that she had agreed to design the girl's costume for free.

Or, rather . . . for a "favor" at some unspecified date. Rhea never did anything for free.

"Hmm . . ." Rhea pondered, tapping her pencil against her cheek. It had a feather taped to the top, because anything she used in view of a customer had to be elegant. "What kind of costume do you think I should design her?"

"Costume?" Chronos asked, sounding startled.

"Defectors always care about costumes," Rhea said, making a broad sketch of an idea she'd been considering a few days ago. "I presume this one came to you because she heard you were related to me."

"No, she doesn't know you exist," Chronos said.

More and more interesting! Rhea kept her glee hidden as she looked up at her sister. "Well, what kind of magical girl outfit did she used to wear?"

Chronos looked blank.

"Are there any elements or motifs that she tends to favor?" Rhea asked patiently.

Chronos continued to look blank.

"Does she have a favorite kind of fabric?" Rhea prodded.

"Um . . . the kind that clothes are made of?"

"Does it *wrinkle,* or is it stiff?" Rhea asked impatiently.

"Oh. Her first magical girl outfit was fluffy and it wrapped around her. Like a bathrobe," Chronos said. "The future one was going to be stiff."

Rhea had extreme doubts that the defector had worn something that resembled a bathrobe. "What else?"

"Um . . . she wears a lot of buckles . . .?" Chronos said.

"Buckles!" Rhea cried in delight. She hadn't been asked to design a villain outfit with buckles in months! She started sketching, singing to herself, "I make vil-lains look the cool-est!"

"*Ngh,*" Chronos muttered behind her.

As she sketched, Rhea cast her mind over magical girl pasts from all over the world, looking for defectors who had worn a lot of buckles, but she couldn't see any. She couldn't see any recent defections at all, actually, and she was very skilled at finding them. Could it be . . .?

Rhea weighed the pros and cons of speaking up, and decided that the chance to pump her sister for more information was more important than refraining from irritating her. After all, Chronos must be pretty desperate, or she wouldn't be here. That meant she wasn't likely to turn and leave.

"Huh. I can't see any recent defections," Rhea said casually, glancing down at her hand. "Were you actually *involved* in this one?"

Chronos glowered. "Much as I appreciate your attempts to spy on me . . ."

"Ha!" Rhea crowed. "So you were!"

"Mind your own business!" Chronos shouted.

Rhea was delighted, but she kept her face composed to hide her glee. This was a wonderful step for her sister, and she knew that smugness would only make her scowl and flee. So she answered in a matter-of-fact tone instead.

"Oh, don't be so huffy," Rhea said. "I can't see your past any more than you can see my future."

"But you would if you could," Chronos accused.

"Of course," Rhea said. "You'd spy on me if you could, too."

Chronos's eyes narrowed, but she didn't deny it.

"Besides, we both know Papa was right," Rhea added briskly, flipping the page to move on to her second sketch. "Magical girls are our natural enemies. Before they came along, all our world's magic-users were mocked, persecuted or killed. But for some reason, everyone reveres *them*. Revered for a magic system that's so overpowered, and with such little cost, it's like cheating! If you've shown even one of them reason to quit, you should be *proud*."

"Like you're proud when you pick fights with them?" Chronos asked flatly.

"Of course," Rhea said, glancing up at her. "They're trouble. Even mages from other worlds are starting to fear them."

"Because they also pick fights with them!" Chronos shouted.

"And rightly so," Rhea said, snapping her fingers. "Minerva!"

Her minion walked through the curtain, letting it swish shut behind her. Her arrowhead-like tail poked out behind her as soon as there were no customers in sight range. "Yes, ma'am?"

At least she has the good sense to make sure the customers don't see it, Rhea thought. She would have preferred her sister to have not known where her minion was from, because information that interesting could be traded for more information, but . . . ah, well. In that case, there was no real point in hiding Minerva's power.

"Make these for me," she said, handing the two sketches to her minion.

Chronos looked restless. "How long will it take? I only have half an hour before she wakes up again, and it's a ten-minute taxi ride from the Deathwave tunnel."

Rhea almost laughed at how easily her sister gave up information. There were only nine Deathwave teleporter tunnels in the world, all between cities with major villain activity. If she hadn't already known her sister lived in Athens, it would have been laughably easy to find her.

Then again, giving her sister the benefit of the doubt, Chronos had most likely assumed that Rhea knew where she lived already. Which was true.

Rhea couldn't automatically find the holes her sister left in the past, unlike finding scenes from anyone else's past, but once she stumbled upon a hole, she could infer plenty. She could always tell the general location where her sister had been, for instance, not to mention when she'd been there, and she could listen to what other people had said about her after she'd left.

Meanwhile, her sister couldn't see any possible futures which involved her, which meant that Chronos had no way of knowing whether she was missing important things or whether there was nothing to see. Chronos couldn't even see possible futures which involved *herself,* which was an added limitation that Rhea didn't have. She could see her own past just fine.

Rhea repressed a smirk.

"Won't take long at all," Minerva said, holding the sketches out on each side of her. "Boss hired me for a reason."

"Because you're fast at sewing?" Chronos asked.

Minerva snorted. "No."

A glow and a river of sparkles spread from each hand, and the tip of a sleeve emerged from one paper.

"Make sure to get both sizes right!" Rhea called.

"If these don't fit, I'm blaming your drawing skills," Minerva shot back.

The spirals spun faster and faster, and lines from the drawings darted out of the paper, forming into edges of real-life cloth as they appeared. As the last of the lines formed into reality, both costumes landed with a heap on the floor.

Chronos's mouth was open.

"You forgot the boots," Rhea said.

Minerva checked both papers. She held one of them upside down and shook it. Glows emerged from that hand as the boots dumped out of the paper onto the floor. She checked both papers to make sure they were blank, and then handed them back over.

"That's an unusual power," Chronos said.

Rhea took the blank papers and tossed them in the trash. They tended to get crumpled when Minerva used them, and paper was cheap.

Minerva snorted and rolled her eyes. "Only around here."

"Around where?" Chronos asked.

Unbelievable, Rhea thought, shaking her head. Her sister hadn't noticed the tail.

Then again, if her sister was really that unobservant . . .

"Go total her purchases," Rhea said pleasantly. "Use the chart for Ultra-Special Tier A customers."

Minerva grinned and ran off, tail bouncing eagerly after her. She got paid on commission, so she loved it when they charged customers the ten-times-normal rate.

Chronos prodded one of the costumes with her foot. "Why'd you make two? She only really needs one."

"The black one's for her; the red one's for you," Rhea said. "Did I get her size right? I assumed average height and weight for a thirteen-year-old — is she thirteen?"

Unfortunately, Chronos didn't take the bait and accidentally volunteer more information.

"You designed a villain outfit for *me?*" Chronos burst out, grabbing the red one and holding it up.

"Well, you're not walking out of my store dressed like *that,*" Rhea said tartly. "I have a reputation to maintain."

"I'm not going to wear this thing!" Chronos shouted.

"Would you rather go home empty-handed?" Rhea asked, holding up the black costume tantalizingly.

Chronos pursed her lips and glared.

Advice, Rhea remembered. *She came looking for advice to get that defector of hers to leave. She's too clueless to understand how important costumes are. She might very well just storm off empty-handed if I don't spell it out for her.*

"Here's my advice," Rhea said gently. "Every new villain needs a costume, lair, arch-nemesis, and ultimate goal. If she's clinging to you, it's probably because she feels she's missing something she needs. This costume might be it."

Chronos hesitated. She seemed to be thinking.

"That'll be $54,739!" Minerva announced cheerfully, bouncing back into the room. "Cash or credit charge?"

"Oh — credit charge," Chronos said. She recited a number.

It was all Rhea could do to keep from laughing as Minerva raced off with gleaming eyes. Chronos was at a shop for villains, and she wasn't supervising the charge to her account? Really?

Her poor little baby sister. Thirty-three, and yet so naive.

Chronos stared at her reflection in the mirror, swallowing. Despite her vigorous protests, her sister had insisted on brushing her hair and shoving her into the dressing room with the red dress. Even though it was now five minutes past when Chronos had wanted to leave, she couldn't quite make herself walk out like this. She'd thought nothing of being seen in public with her pajamas and bunny slippers, but this . . .

I look like a villain, she thought queasily. *I don't want to look like a villain.*

But if she didn't wear this, her sister wouldn't let her leave. And if she didn't leave, Kendra would wake up, find her gone, and no doubt teleport to wherever Chronos was currently.

She'd worked so hard to convince Kendra that she wasn't a villain. If Kendra showed up here, she'd figure out that Chronos had come from a villain family, which was the last thing she wanted that annoying pest to realize.

Besides, that wasn't the only reason she wanted to leave before Kendra woke up and chased her here.

Kendra had a chip on her shoulder about corrupt magical girls.

Rhea's favorite hobby was corrupting magical girls.

Somehow, that didn't seem like a meeting she wanted to see.

Showing up wearing this isn't going to convince the pest that I'm not a villain, Chronos thought gloomily. *Although . . . I guess . . . I could wear this long enough to take Rhea's advice . . .*

If Rhea was right, it wasn't just a costume Kendra would need.

From a distance, she heard her sister shout, "Minerva! She's family! *Only* triple-charge it!"

Chronos walked into the living room, dumped the villain costume on her unwanted houseguest's face, and said, "Hi, Kendra. If you still want to be a villain, here's your costume."

"*Mmph!*" Kendra yelped, waking up under the fabric.

Chronos grinned at the revenge. It was nice to be the one to wake the pest up this time.

"We'll go shopping for a lair in half an hour," she announced carelessly, marching past the couch towards her bedroom. "Get dressed in time for that, or get out."

She knew of several villain realtors in the city. Her family had bought properties from several of them while she was a kid.

Chapter 3
The Realtor

Costume, Kendra thought, hugging the fabric, smelling its fresh new-clothing scent. *I have a costume again.*

About the only thing that had kept her together the past few days had been her determination. Now that it seemed she'd won . . . she wasn't sure what to think.

A costume again. That was a start. She had a costume. That felt like getting back half of what she'd lost.

Except . . . I can't transform anymore, Kendra thought, staring at it. Tears rose in her eyes, and she blinked them back. *This will never become a second life. It's only cloth. If someone had killed Cream Angel, I would just have lost my powers. But now . . .*

Now, if I ever lose a battle . . . I'll die.

She set the costume carefully beside her, looking at it. Taking it in. It was black and sleeveless, with a white border around the neck and down the front. It had a short skirt and a silver belt with a trapezoid-shaped bronze buckle.

It was an awesome buckle.

A very awesome buckle.

I could wear this, Kendra thought, imagining it on herself. *This could be my style as a villain.*

A lump rose in her throat.

The Realtor

I've killed villains before. Now I'm one of them. I'm going to be battling without a second life to shield me, and I'm going to be fighting those I used to revere.

It begged a question she didn't want to know the answer to.

Does that make me a hypocrite, or just plain vulnerable?

"And here's a lovely place for any villain just starting out!" the realtor proclaimed, waving her hand dramatically. A cloud of darkness swirled before them, revealing . . .

. . . a three-towered building in very poor repair.

"Really?" Kendra muttered.

There were visible bricks all over the walls, even though it had been painted to cover them. Three times, at least, judging by how many different colors of paint were visible in peeling layers. Despite its size, the building had only five windows, all of them near the top, and they were all enormous, which meant it would be uncomfortable to live in and impractical to defend.

And then there was the fact that the enormous building was all by itself on top of a hill, with nothing else around for miles. A more conspicuous lair there could not possibly be.

"Yes, a perfect lair for anyone who really wants to be found," Kendra said sarcastically.

The realtor's chipper attitude seemed unchanged. "Only if they invite other people here, such as villains they want to impress! The whole building is covered by anti-tracking magic barriers!"

Chronos's eyebrows raised. She looked impressed.

"The building, but not the grounds?" Kendra asked suspiciously.

"The barrier extends a whole foot outside the walls!" the realtor said cheerfully.

Kendra snorted. *In other words, completely useless if you go outside for any reason.* "Next," she said.

"Oh, you will love this building!" the realtor enthused as if she hadn't heard, skipping ahead of them across the straggly grass. "It's absolutely perfect for your needs!"

Chronos ambled after her, and Kendra hurried to catch up.

"This is the seventh trash heap she's dragged us to," Kendra muttered in an undertone. "Why are we doing this?"

"New villains need lairs," Chronos shrugged.

"What was wrong with your apartment?" Kendra asked.

"The fact that I don't want you using it as a lair," Chronos said through clenched teeth.

Kendra rolled her eyes. *A lair that doesn't look like a lair would be good camouflage. Okay, the apartment would have been lame, but at least it wasn't a horrendous ripoff. Five of the buildings we've looked at today have had broken walls, and one of them still had the previous owner's dead body in it!*

The realtor's unbelievable reaction to that particular discovery had been to say cheerfully, "As you can see, this property is in such high demand that it's always snapped up almost immediately! Better move fast — it's been on the market for two days, and I guarantee it'll be snapped up before it's been vacant for three!"

As if the corpse in the main hallway had been some sort of selling point or something.

"We can't trust a word she says," Kendra hissed. "I know for a fact that she's lied to us about several things already."

"She's a realtor for villains," Chronos shrugged. "You expected honesty?"

"There have to be better realtors out there!" Kendra hissed.

"If by 'better' you mean more effective at lying to people and stealing their money, then yes, there are. I can take us to an agency that specializes in breaking into already-occupied lairs and selling them to new owners, for instance."

"Villains," Kendra muttered.

Chronos smirked. "Regretting changing your allegiance? It's not too late to back out."

"No," Kendra said immediately.

The realtor pranced straight through an arched doorway at the front of the building. Kendra and Chronos followed her through the gaping archway, which led straight to an entryway.

"Have you noticed there's no front door?" Kendra asked.

"It doesn't need one!" the realtor exclaimed in a thrilled voice. "The archway's automatic defenses only let in people who have been invited in! It's very convenient!"

"Then how did you get in?" Kendra demanded. "How did *we* get in?"

"The agency owns the property, so I qualify as one living here!" the realtor said cheerfully.

"Is there a dead body in here, too?" Kendra demanded.

"This whole place is *so beautiful!*" the realtor exclaimed, prancing down the hallway. "Just wait, you'll love it!"

Kendra put up with the overly-superlative sales pitch with her usual grumpy suspicion as the realtor led them through the rooms along the top floor. It didn't seem as bad as she'd expected, though. There were no dead bodies, all the walls seemed intact, and the only red flag she saw was that there was a huge layer of dust covering everything.

Everything.

Including the bannister of the stairs.

How long has this lair sat vacant? Kendra wondered.

"So here we have a sweeping staircase, leading down to a vast entrance . . ." the realtor said, skipping down the stairs and waving around at the cavernous room beneath them. "Fully-furnished plotting room . . . picturesque bedrooms . . . state-of-the-art bathrooms . . ."

The "fully-furnished" plotting room had one long table, twelve chairs, and a chalkboard that was three times larger than anything Kendra had seen at school.

The "picturesque" bedrooms on the top floor had a superb view through the giant windows of absolutely nothing but empty, scrubby hills.

The plumbing barely worked in one of the "state-of-the-art" bathrooms, and another one had rusted fixtures. On the other hand, all three had an enormous flat-screen TV attached to the wall next to the bathtub.

Somebody had strange priorities, Kendra thought, shaking her head.

Still . . . the walls were intact, there were no corpses anywhere, and overall, it seemed head and shoulders better than anything else they'd see today.

"So what do you think?" the realtor asked breathlessly, beaming as she led them back into the cavernous open space that the stairs led down to.

"Actually . . . this place isn't half-bad," Kendra admitted. She glanced over at Chronos. "I wonder what the catch it?"

"Probably cost," Chronos said, glancing upward. "Did you notice there's a chandelier in this room?"

Kendra snorted. "Somehow, I'm sure price won't be the only problem."

"And finally, the dungeons!" the realtor's voice called from behind them. There was a sound of a door opening, then quickly slamming.

Kendra and Chronos spun to look in that direction.

"The door to which . . . uh . . . seems to be stuck . . ." the realtor said nervously.

"Catch?" Kendra asked Chronos.

"Catch," Chronos confirmed.

"No! Wait!" the realtor cried.

"Good villains need good dungeons," Kendra said darkly. "Aren't those one of the key features of a lair?"

"Why won't this door open?!" the realtor wailed, placing her foot on the door and pulling on it.

So that's why this place has sat empty for so long, Kendra thought with a smirk. *What villain would buy a place with dungeons they can't reach?*

"Actually . . . this place seems adequate," Chronos spoke up. "If lack of dungeons are the only problem, we'll take it."

The realtor was by her side in a flash. "Terrific! Here's a contract! Don't bother to read it before you sign!"

"Soothsayer!" Kendra shouted. "Are you *crazy?*"

Chronos took the contract, carelessly signed two copies without reading them, wrote down her account number, and handed over one of the copies. The realtor was brimming with joy.

The Realtor

Kendra watched in indignant disbelief.

"Are we done here?" Chronos asked, capping the pen.

"I have some lovely extra perks that you can —!"

"No," Chronos said flatly. "I'm done shopping. You can go now."

"So pleased to make your acquaintance!" the realtor sang, skipping up the stairs in sheer ebullience.

Bad, bad, bad, bad, BAD MOVE! Kendra thought furiously.

The realtor exploded from the lair, giddy with her success. She'd known as soon as she'd seen those two that they'd be the perfect marks. Their costumes had been brand new, their faces unfamiliar, and they'd had no affiliation with the Deathwaves.

She'd been banking on the hope that they might not have heard the rumors about that particular property, and she'd been right. She still couldn't believe how perfectly it had gone, even though she'd nearly messed up. In all the heat of her excitement, she'd completely lost her head and nearly shown them the dungeons.

But the older one had been a sucker, through and through. She hadn't even looked at the contract. All that effort to carefully obfuscate the meaning of the third page hadn't even been necessary!

She grinned so brightly that it hurt her cheeks, and yanked a bricklike object from her pocket as she raced down the hill. It was a cellular phone, an incredibly expensive luxury, but one the agency provided for all of their top sellers as a way to make sure that they had a way to call for help in case one of their satisfied customers attempted to kill them.

"Guess what, Marnie?" she shouted into the phone. "It's Valancy! They *bought* it!"

From the scream of fury, she knew that her coworker was slightly discontented that Valancy had successfully sold the property that none of the rest of them had succeeded in getting rid of.

I wonder how long they'll still be alive, the realtor thought, grinning broadly. *How long will it be before I can sell it again?*

She'd had to sell it six times over the past three years, which was twice as often as any other lair their agency took hold of, and after it had sat empty for the past half a year, she'd started to think she'd never find another buyer clueless enough to purchase it. But she just had.

The only thing that would make this perfect is if the buyer doesn't have the money in cash, and so has to go with a mortgage, Valancy thought gleefully. *Which they can only do through our bank. If that's the case, the agency will be able to confiscate every penny they owned when they die.*

And of course realtors got paid on commission for that.

Valancy Darkwater loved her job. She didn't have to have magic to be a villain.

Chapter 4
The Catch

You bought it," Kendra moaned, smacking her face into her hands. "You actually bought it."

"I was tired of shopping," Chronos said. "You liked it fine, didn't you?"

"Before I found out that the dungeons don't work!" Kendra shot back. "Not to mention whatever else is wrong with it that the realtor was hiding!"

Chronos shrugged. "There'll be something wrong with every lair. You'll never find an honest villain realtor. At least here, we knew exactly what the problem was, and it wasn't a big deal."

"Not a big deal?" Kendra asked incredulously. "A complete lack of dungeons, not a big deal?"

"*I'm* not planning to use dungeons for anything," Chronos said. "Are *you*?"

Kendra sputtered, seeming to be caught by the obvious logic.

"Well, of course not, but don't you know the first thing about bargaining?" the former magical girl burst out at last. "You could have used that obvious problem to ask for a better price! How much did you *pay*?"

"Good question," Chronos said, shuffling through the papers. "I didn't look."

"You *DIDN'T LOOK?!*"

"It wasn't like I was going to prolong the conversation by arguing over it," Chronos said. She was starting to feel pretty annoyed over the pest's ingratitude. "Whatever it was, I could pay it. Ah, here it is."

She found the relevant paper in the stack. The purchase price had been buried in the middle of an exceptionally boring paragraph, written in very small print. Chronos gave the number a cursory glance to make sure she had enough money in her account to cover it without a mortgage — she did — and held the paper out for Kendra to see.

Kendra snatched the paper, her voice rising in a shrill scream. "How could you afford a number with *EIGHT ZEROES?!*"

Chronos shrugged. "I day-traded stocks for a few weeks, several years ago."

It had been quite unpleasant. She'd had to talk to people over the phone, sign papers in person, and interact with extremely intense individuals over and over again. Still, it had been worth it, given that the easy-to-earn money had bought her a ticket to successfully ignoring the world for the next seven years.

Come to think of it, Chronos thought, *perhaps I shouldn't have given my account number to someone who'd feel no guilt whatsoever about clearing it out?*

Whatever. She still had her backup account. It'd be a minor nuisance if her main account had been compromised irreparably, but not enough to necessitate bothering to do anything about it.

Kendra stared at her with narrowed eyes. "*Someone* uses her magic for personal gain . . ."

"I've never seen a problem with that," Chronos said.

Kendra's jaw twitched. "Magic is supposed to be used for higher purposes. For saving the world."

"And yet, somehow, the world survived," Chronos said flatly.

Kendra seemed to be struggling with her temper. She tossed the paper back to Chronos, who made no attempt to catch it, so it flipped through the air, spun the wrong direction, and landed on top of one of Kendra's feet.

Chronos's lips curved upwards in amusement.

Kendra's jaw twitched again.

"Whatever," she said. "When do we move in? Can you pack everything by today?"

Chronos stared at the former magical girl.

"What?" Kendra asked.

Chronos just kept staring at her.

"*What?*" Kendra demanded.

"*We* do not move in," Chronos said, turning her back and heading towards the stairs. "This lair is *yours*. Enjoy."

"Are you *seriously* planning to go back to that lame apartment after buying this place?" the former magical girl burst out from behind her.

"It isn't like I'm short on money," Chronos said, putting her hand on the bannister of the stairs. "I just wanted my privacy back."

Her fingers left a trail across the bannister, which was shiny underneath all that blanket of grey fuzz.

Huh, Chronos thought. *I didn't even notice there was dust.*

She rarely noticed such things. She hadn't even been aware that the top of the stove in her apartment's kitchen had been covered with dust until Kendra had made a really big deal about it. *"Do you never cook?! How long has it been since you touched that thing?!"*

Which was silly, since of course Chronos cooked. She cooked premade meals. She had a microwave.

"That's completely ridiculous," Kendra sputtered. "I don't need a gigantic building all to myself. Besides, what am I supposed to do? Teleport to your place every day?"

Chronos felt a stab of annoyance. "No. You're supposed to *not* teleport to my apartment every day."

Kendra snorted. "Well, it'll be pretty hard to coordinate our plans of attack if I don't. You don't own a phone."

Chronos stared at her incredulously. Was the pest really so blindly stubborn that she'd missed the obvious point that Chronos had been trying to make? That Chronos had, in fact, outright stated over and over again?

"We're not going to coordinate any plans of attack," Chronos said. "We are not teammates."

"You don't get a choice in that matter, soothsayer," Kendra said.

Chronos exploded. "Don't you understand why I bought this lair? I want you to stay *here,* while I go *there.* I want you to leave me alone!"

"Not gonna happen," Kendra said.

"Yes, it is!" Chronos shouted. "I'm not going to give you any information! I'm not going to tell you anything! You'll never get a word out of me!"

Kendra sighed. "Are you saying that I'll have to eavesdrop on you while you sleep? That seems really roundabout and inconvenient to me. Plus pretty boring."

Chronos stared at the stubborn pest in absolute disbelief. Was this the personality of a person who had been destined to found the Magical Girl Union at age seventeen, start several wars at eighteen, and destroy the world before she was nineteen?

No wonder no one in the future had been able to talk reason into this girl. It was impossible.

"Now," Kendra said reasonably, "if you willingly give me the information I want whenever I want it, that's a whole lot less time you'll have to spend with me. I don't expect you to fight magical girls, and I don't expect us to be friends. I only ask that you help me save the world."

"You're not asking," Chronos muttered. *"Asking* means you're willing to accept 'no.'"

"True," Kendra said.

Chronos clenched her jaw. There was only one thing she was certain about right now, and that was that giving this girl the teleporting watch had been a major mistake. If she could have only seen her own futures, she would have known that.

"Of course, it will make much more sense for you to move in here," Kendra said briskly. "I'm sure there will be people looking for us both eventually, and anti-tracking magic barriers will be useful to keep them out."

Chronos stared at the former magical girl in horror. It had never occurred to her that there might be *other people* tracking her, too. Other people besides Kendra. Other people who might be converging on Chronos's home already.

She would definitely have to move. Perhaps to another city.

Probably one with Deathwave teleporter tubes, so she could escape easily. That meant Paris, Athens, Nairobi, Moscow, Hong Kong, Melbourne, New York, Rio de Janeiro, or Mexico City.

Of course, those were all cities known for major villain activity. Which meant those were the first places anyone would look for her.

Blast it, Chronos thought furiously. *I should never have given up that watch.*

"I'm not staying," Chronos said. "I'm not giving you any information. I just want to get rid of you. Do you want me to pay you to go away? How much will it take?"

"Stop trying to get rid of me!" Kendra exclaimed. "I didn't come to you for *money* — I want a team I can trust!"

"The money, I can provide," Chronos said coldly. "That's it."

There was silence as Kendra glared at her. Chronos stared frostily back.

The silence stretched on, and on, and on.

"Oracle . . . I can't save the world on my own," Kendra said quietly. "If I could, I would have been a solo magical girl. I always wanted to make a difference, but it wasn't until we started a team that I started to think think we could do great things."

Chronos said nothing. She kept silent.

"I need a team," Kendra said. "Right now, there's nobody I can trust but you. I certainly can't go to any other villains."

Chronos said nothing.

"Florence and Felicity wouldn't have stopped me," Kendra said, tears glinting at the edge of her eyes. "Neither would my parents. If they could have, you wouldn't have shown me that future."

Chronos hesitated. Had there been futures in which Kendra's family and friends could have stopped her? She'd never thought to check. She'd cared only about the worst case scenario, not the natural solutions that might have existed.

She'd been determined to excise that future from existing altogether. And she had. Now that it was gone, she had no way to check what might have been if she had left Cream Angel alone. She did know there had been futures without such problems.

If she'd paid more attention, if she had been more careful, she could have found a way to divert that future until it was vanishingly unlikely, without shocking or traumatizing anybody. She could have fixed the problem more subtly.

But Chronos didn't understand subtlety. Chronos didn't *do* subtlety. The only person who could have come up with a plan like that would have been Rhea. And Rhea would, undoubtably, have made the future much worse.

A subtle plan from Rhea, who adored corrupting magical girls . . . Chronos shuddered at even the thought of it. She might have taken a sledgehammer to Kendra's future, but at least she hadn't unleashed her sister into it.

"That's why I had to leave," Kendra said. One of the tears trickled down the side of her face. "That's why I had to burn my bridges. I had to prevent my fate."

Did she think it was inevitable? Chronos wondered, alarmed. *I never said that — in fact, I did say that it was only a likely future.*

"You — you didn't have to leave," Chronos said hesitantly. "It was only a likely future. You could have stayed —"

Kendra brushed that objection aside with an angry wave of her hand. "With the *whole world* at stake? Of course I had to make that future impossible!"

Chronos swallowed. That was how she'd felt about going to talk to Kendra in the first place. When the stakes were that high, any chance of that future happening was not okay.

"I need a team," Kendra repeated. "Besides, after what you showed me . . . well, I think I need someone to keep me under control."

Chronos felt a flash of anger. *If you would just control yourself, that wouldn't be a problem!*

But Kendra was no longer talking. She just stood there, looking vulnerable.

You're just trying to manipulate me, Chronos thought furiously. *My sister used to use that trick on me constantly!*

Except that . . . in all of Kendra's futures she'd seen, the girl had never done that. She had been glorious or dreadful, protected innocents or killed them, destroyed the world or saved it.

She had never, ever looked weak.

Which means it's . . . real? Chronos thought.

The thought was frightening. More frightening than the idea of strangers chasing her all over the world. More frightening than the idea of never having privacy again.

Because if it was real, then she might have to do something about it.

Chronos drew in a deep breath and let it out again.

"Are you saying you want me to be your boss?" she asked slowly.

Kendra snorted. "It's not like I could trust *myself* to lead a new team." Her voice was bitter.

Her boss, Chronos thought, amazed. *She has a bizarre way of recruiting someone to be her boss.*

She couldn't deny that the idea had some appeal. She'd never been in charge of anybody or anything. All her life, people had been telling her what to do and how to use her power to benefit themselves. She'd grown extremely sick of it.

Her boss . . .

Chronos pondered the idea for a moment. It was almost tempting, save for one thing: Kendra's refusal to accept the answer of "no."

It's not an empowering situation to be forced into a position of authority! Chronos thought indignantly.

"I need you," Kendra said again. "You're the only person I can trust in the world. I need you to help me, and I might need you to stop me."

Chronos hunched her shoulders. She couldn't believe she was being put in this position.

"But I still don't want . . ." she began.

Scritch scratch crack BANG "OW!" a voice shouted from the distance.

Chronos whirled around, looking around wildly for the source of the unknown voice. Was someone invisible in here with them?

"Hey, minions! Do you have any band-aids?" the muffled voice shouted, coming from beneath them. "Oh, wait, never mind, duct tape will work!"

Chronos was dumbfounded. *Who in the world . . .?*

"Who said that?!" Kendra shouted, her voice sharp and angry. All traces of her former vulnerability were gone.

"I diiiiiiiiiiiiiiiid!" the voice called from downstairs. The voice's high pitch and singsong tone made it sound like it belonged to a little girl.

A little girl, Chronos thought, baffled. *Why would there be a little girl here? No villain would keep a little girl in their lair, unless . . .*

The realization came crashing down on her.

Kendra flipped through the pages of the contract from the realtor, stopping to poke a tiny clause buried in the middle.

"There." She smirked and held it out for Chronos to see. "You really should have read that contract before you signed."

"The dungeons *came* with a *prisoner?*" Chronos shouted.

"Hey, Baron Deathwave, is that you?" the little girl voice called cheerfully from downstairs. "I built that brainwasher you wanted!"

A brainwasher. Chronos sat on the stairs and buried her face in her hands. *That's all we need: a device to turn magical girls or innocent bystanders into temporary minions. Why on Earth would a prisoner build one?*

"Good job finding such a great deal," Kendra chortled. "You didn't have to bargain — the realtor threw in a prisoner for free!"

Chronos moaned and buried her face further in her hands.

"C'mon, we'd better find out who our new teammate is," Kendra said.

Chronos's hands flew off her face. "No!" she shouted. "I am not your teammate, and I am certainly not anyone else's!"

"That's a little rude, given that you haven't even met our new teammate yet," Kendra said, smirking.

Chronos glowered at her.

"I assume there's a key somewhere," Kendra added, wandering over to the wooden door that the realtor had wrestled with and found impossible to open. "Unless, of course, the realtor was just pretending that it was stuck . . ."

It'll be stuck, Chronos thought. *It'll definitely be stuck. That's the only reason why there would still be a prisoner here.*

The Catch

After all, prisoners were considered a valuable resource. At the very least, the realtor would have collected a prisoner and auctioned them off to the highest bidder, to be used as a hostage or minion.

It made no *sense* for there to be a prisoner here if the dungeons were accessible.

Kendra lifted the wooden latch, and the door slid open smoothly.

"Yep, we've been had!" she called, dancing down the stairs. "This door works perfectly!"

Chronos's stomach sank. There was only one reason she could think of to leave a prisoner behind, and that was if the prisoner was dangerous. So dangerous than no villains wanted them.

Who was in their dungeons, and what was waiting for them?